YOU CAN'T GO TO SCHOOL NAKED!

by **Dianne Billstrom**
illustrated by **Don Kilpatrick III**

G. P. PUTNAM'S SONS

G. P. PUTNAM'S SONS. A division of Penguin Young Readers Group. Published by The Penguin Group. Penguin Group (USA) Inc., 375 Hudson Street, New York, NY 10014, U.S.A. Penguin Group (Canada), 90 Eglinton Avenue East, Suite 700, Toronto, Ontario M4P 2Y3, Canada (a division of Pearson Penguin Canada Inc.). Penguin Books Ltd, 80 Strand, London WC2R 0RL, England. Penguin Ireland, 25 St. Stephen's Green, Dublin 2, Ireland (a division of Penguin Books Ltd.). Penguin Group (Australia), 250 Camberwell Road, Camberwell, Victoria 3124, Australia (a division of Pearson Australia Group Pty Ltd). Penguin Books India Pvt Ltd, 11 Community Centre, Panchsheel Park, New Delhi - 110 017, India. Penguin Group (NZ), 67 Apollo Drive, Rosedale, North Shore 0632, New Zealand (a division of Pearson New Zealand Ltd.). Penguin Books (South Africa) (Pty) Ltd, 24 Sturdee Avenue, Rosebank, Johannesburg 2196, South Africa. Penguin Books Ltd, Registered Offices: 80 Strand, London WC2R 0RL, England. Text copyright © 2008 by Dianne Billstrom. Illustrations copyright © 2008 by Don Kilpatrick III. All rights reserved. This book, or parts thereof, may not be reproduced in any form without permission in writing from the publisher, G. P. Putnam's Sons, a division of Penguin Young Readers Group, 345 Hudson Street, New York, NY 10014. G. P. Putnam's Sons, Reg. U.S. Pat. & Tm. Off. The scanning, uploading and distribution of this book via the Internet or via any other means without the permission of the publisher is illegal and punishable by law. Please purchase only authorized electronic editions, and do not participate in or encourage electronic piracy of copyrighted materials. Your support of the author's rights is appreciated. The publisher does not have any control over and does not assume any responsibility for author or third-party websites or their content. Published simultaneously in Canada. Manufactured in China by South China Printing Co. Ltd. Design by Richard Amari. Text set in Klepto and Skippy Sharp. The art was created using acrylic on Strathmore 500 series illustration board. Library of Congress Cataloging-in-Publication Data. Billstrom, Dianne. You can't go to school naked! / Dianne Billstrom ; illustrated by Don Kilpatrick. p. cm. Summary: Parents warn their son of all the dangers he may encounter if he goes to school without wearing clothes. [1. Nudity—Fiction. 2. Clothing and dress—Fiction. 3. Schools—Fiction. 4. Stories in rhyme.] I. Kilpatrick, Don, ill. II. Title. III. Title: You cannot go to school naked! PZ8.3.B4948Yo 2008 [E]—dc22 2007027891 ISBN 978-0-399-24738-5 10 9 8 7 6 5 4 3 2

"*I must wear clothes? That's what you say?*
*I don't **LIKE** clothes! I say—**NO WAY!**"*

You can't go to school naked! That is a rule.
You must wear clothes when you go to school!

What would you do with no pockets for things,
like pencil stubs, marbles, and sprocket springs?

If you went to school naked, your teacher would think
you must be a pig, all bristly and pink!

Being a pig, all bristly and pink,
you'd roll in the mud. Phew! You would stink!

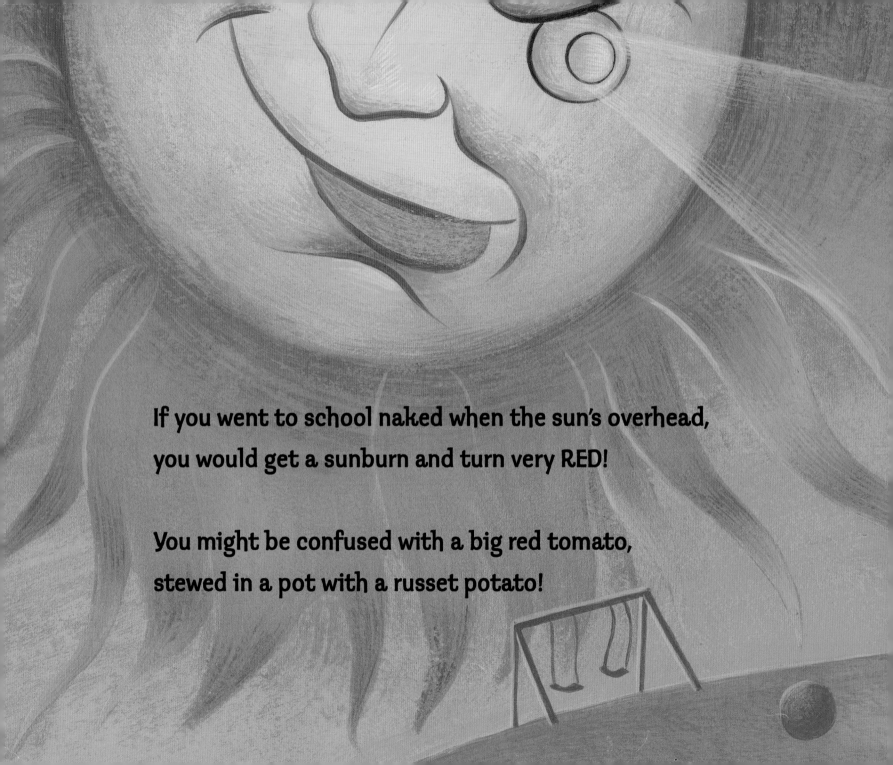

If you went to school naked when the sun's overhead,
you would get a sunburn and turn very RED!

You might be confused with a big red tomato,
stewed in a pot with a russet potato!

Without your clothes, in winter you'd freeze.
Your skin would turn blue. There'd be frost to your knees!

You should wear clothes to stay warm and snug.
You could get sick—catch a flu bug!

While at an easel with brush and paint,
or finger painting without constraint,

not wearing clothing isn't too smart.
You could become your own work of art!

If you went to school naked, could you play ball?

Steal second base? NO, not at all!

On the playground if you slipped down the slide,
without your clothes you'd have quite a ride.

Especially near summer, with your exposed hide,
you'd come out all crispy, like being French-fried!

During show-and-tell, what would you do
if a toad or snail was handed to you?

They tend to like to creep and to climb—
you could become a huge mass of SLIME!

You can't go to school naked! Come to your senses!

Consider, if you please, the consequences.

"Is it true? Is it true? What they have said?"
he began to mumble as he crawled into bed.

His mind was racing through muddy pigsties,
simmering stews—even slime in his eyes!

He tossed and turned so much in his dream,
by the time he woke, he'd thought of a scheme.

"As long as I'm covered, you say I can't lose.
If I have to wear clothes, here's what I choose!"